Percy
to the Rescue

Story by Diana Noonan
Illustrations by James Hart

Contents

Chapter 1
A New Pet

On Monday afternoon, Tom sat in the back of Mrs. Judd's taxi van with a big grin on his face.

He couldn't wait to get home from school.

"You sure look excited about something," said Mrs. Judd, as she parked outside Tom's house.

"I am," replied Tom. "My family is getting a new pet. He's a parrot called Percy. He'll be waiting for me when I get inside."

Mrs. Judd helped Tom wheel his chair out of the taxi.

"Mom and Dad and I are going to teach Percy to talk," said Tom.

"Have fun together!" said Mrs. Judd, as she drove away.

Tom's mom and dad worked from home. They were writers.
But when Tom went inside,
Mom and Dad weren't in their office.

They were sitting in front of a big cage in the lounge room.
Inside the cage was Percy.

"Present for Percy!" said Mom, as she fed seeds to the parrot.
"Present for Percy!"

"Hello, Percy!" said Tom.

"Pretty boy!" said Dad to Percy. "Pretty boy!"

"Can he say anything yet?" asked Tom.

"The pet shop people said it could take a few weeks before he talks," said Mom.

"We have to be very patient," added Dad.
"And talk to him a lot."

Chapter 2

Clever Boy!

For three weeks, Mom, Dad, and Tom
talked to Percy all the time.
Percy pretended not to take any notice.
But he did like watching TV.

Percy's favorite program was *Police Patrol*.
When the police cars raced along the highway
with their sirens going, Percy took extra notice.

And after three weeks, Percy began to talk!
He said his first words on Monday morning.

Tom was eating breakfast with Mom and Dad
before he went to school.

Suddenly, Percy said, "Hello! Hello!"

Tom dropped his spoon. Dad stopped chewing his cereal.
Mom almost spilled her coffee.

"Pretty boy! Pretty boy!" said Percy.

"Clever boy!" said Tom.

"Clever boy!" said Percy, right back to him.

Outside, Mrs. Judd tooted the taxi van's horn.

"Off you go to school," said Mom to Tom.

"I want to stay home and listen to Percy," said Tom. "I don't want to go to school!"

"Go to school! Go to school!" squawked Percy.

Everyone looked at the cage. Then they all started laughing.

Chapter 3

Sssh!

By the end of the week,
Percy's chatter wasn't so funny any more.

On Friday night, Dad said, "I can't hear the radio
when Percy is talking all the time."

"He's been copying the ringtone on my cell phone," said Mom.
"Every time I go to answer the phone, no one is there."

"Percy woke us up around midnight last night," said Dad.

"We thought we heard the alarm clock," said Mom.
"Then we found the 'alarm' was coming from Percy's cage!"

"At least he's quiet when the TV is on," said Tom.
"Percy really likes watching TV."

"TV! TV!" squawked Percy.

By Sunday afternoon, Percy had learned
how to make doorbell sounds.

"I go to the door, but no one is there!" said Tom.

On Sunday night, Mom said, "I can hear a rumble.
Who turned on the washing machine?"

But the rumble was coming from Percy!

On Monday morning at breakfast,
Mrs. Judd's taxi horn went *beep beep*.

"I'm sure it's not taxi time yet," said Dad.
"It's not even eight o'clock."

Then everyone looked at Percy.

"Uh oh!" said Tom. "Percy can make *beep beep* noises!"

Chapter 4

Problems with Percy

When Tom came home from school on Friday, Mom and Dad looked very worried.

"What's wrong?" asked Tom.

"We can't get any work done," said Mom. "Percy talks non-stop all day."

"Percy is a big problem," said Dad, anxiously.

"Percy is a problem!" squawked Percy.

"Let's all go for a walk to the park," said Mom.
"It's quiet at the park. We can talk about Percy there."

Dad put Percy back in his cage.
"Be a good boy!" he said, as everyone went out the door.

"Be a good boy!" squawked Percy.

At the park, Mom and Dad said that Percy would have to go back to the pet shop.

"We can't think when he talks so much," said Mom.

"Percy is a nice parrot," said Dad, "but he's not the pet for us."

Tom felt so sad, he thought he might cry.
All the way home from the park,
he tried to think of a way that Percy could stay.

Tom was still thinking hard when they arrived home. He saw that the front door was wide open.

"I know I shut that door!" said Dad.

Suddenly, two men came running out of the house and down the front path.
They almost knocked Mom and Dad over.

"Hey!" shouted Dad.
"What do you think you're doing?"

Mom and Dad rushed up the path and into the house.
Tom was right behind them.

In the hallway was a big pile of things:
the TV, Mom's handbag, Tom's computer,
and Dad's golf clubs.

"We've been burgled!" said Mom.

"Almost burgled," said Dad.

"But what scared the burglars away?" asked Tom.

Before anyone could answer,
a loud police siren began to wail.

The noise was coming from the kitchen.

Chapter 5
Parrot Protection

Everyone went into the kitchen.

"It's Percy!" said Mom.
"He's making those police siren noises
that he copied from the TV!"

"So that's what scared the burglars away!" said Dad.
"Good parrot, Percy!"

"Percy must have learned siren sounds from *Police Patrol,*" said Mom. "It's his favorite TV program."

"I told you Percy was a clever parrot," said Tom.

"We can't send Percy back to the pet shop, now," said Tom. "He's a very useful parrot."

"But how can we work when he talks all day?" asked Mom.

"I know!" said Tom. "Percy is silent when he's watching a TV program. When you and Dad are working, Percy can watch television!"

"Now, that's an idea!" said Dad.

"Good thinking!" agreed Mom.

Tom couldn't stop smiling.

"What do you think about that, Percy?" he asked.

"TV!" squawked Percy, as he ran up and down his perch. "TV for me! TV for me!"

"Coming right up!" said Tom.

And everyone laughed.